# DON'T Chew the Royal Shoe!

Footman's Brogues

Kate Leake

ALISON GREEN BOOKS

Lord Chippington Marmaduke Fluffy Toes
(or Chips, for short) wasn't quite like
the other royal dogs.

He never wanted to chew any of the proper
Royal Chewy Toys in the Queen's splendid palace.

Squeak!
Squook!

He didn't like
the squeaky crown,

Nelleeeaay!

or the plastic pony,

Puhh!

SQUONK!

or even the cuddly corgi.

Unfortunately, the only thing
Chips ever wanted to do was . . .

# . . . chew the Royal Shoes!

"Bad show!"
said the Duke.

"Simply horrid!"
said the Queen.

# Poor Chips!

He really wanted to be a good royal dog, but shoes were just
so CHEWY! Their lovely laces were like spaghetti.
And each shoe had such a delicious smell!

So, each morning, Chips would sneak off very secretly to find another shoe to chew.

He was a very kind dog, though, so he only took one shoe from every pair.

He hid his wonderful shoes
beneath the royal rhododendrons so that he
could chew them whenever he wanted to.
He had lots of favourites.

The Queen's shoe,
which smelled like English roses.

The Princess's glass slipper
– nice and crunchy!

The Duke's roller skate
– super speedy and
fun to chase.

The gardener's wellington boot
– extra muddy, with bonus worms!

Very soon, Chips had chewed his way through
the entire royal shoe collection.

The royal footmen had to
hop around, trying to hide
their holey socks.

The princess had
to go dancing in
one tango shoe.

And the Queen had no matching shoes to wear to the Royal Garden Party.
"What is One to do, without One's other shoe?!"
she exclaimed.

Later that afternoon,
at the Royal Garden Party,
the Queen greeted her guests, wearing
a flip-flop and a wellington boot.

It was **terribly embarrassing.**

And when the Queen inspected the Royal Guards,
she decided that something had to be done.

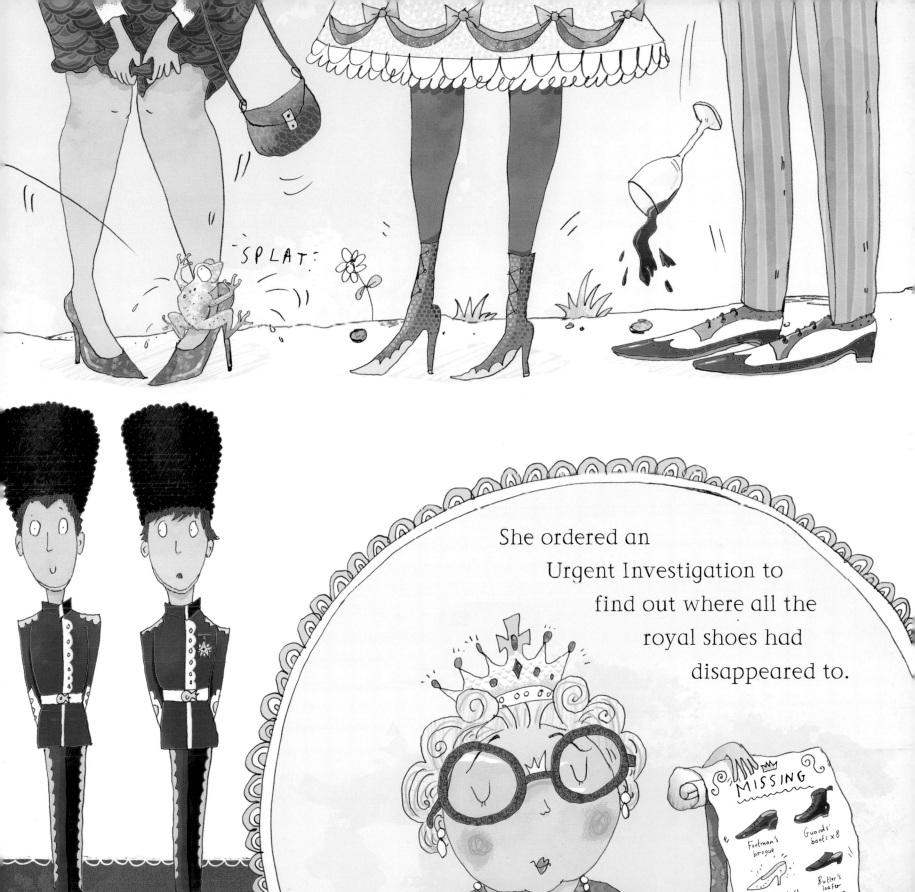

SPLAT

She ordered an
Urgent Investigation to
find out where all the
royal shoes had
disappeared to.

MISSING

Footman's brogue

Guards' boots x8

Princess's glass slipper

Butler's loafer

One's shoe

Coronation sandal

It wasn't long before the royal gardener made a grand discovery – Chips's secret shoe stash!

The gardener told the cook.

The cook told the footman.

ROYAL PIE

The footman told
the butler.

The butler
told the maid,

and the
maid told the
Queen.

The Queen was not amused. Her best slipper was full of holes and her coronation sandal was in shreds.

"One is most DISAPPOINTED, Lord Chippington!"

The Queen ordered her servants to put every shoe in the whole palace well out of reach.

She told Chips that he must only chew the proper Royal Chewy Toys in future.
Then she took away his crown, and sent him to bed with no dinner.

Chips heaved a huge doggie sigh.
He tried nibbling a cuddly corgi,
but it just wasn't the same.

At last, Chips went to sleep
and dreamed about beautiful shoes.
Shiny shoes that smelled of boot polish.

Stinky shoes
that tasted cheesy.

And the Queen's shoes
that smelled like
English roses.

But in the night, while the palace was sleeping, Chips suddenly woke up. His royal doggie ears heard a strange and curious C-R-E-A-K!

His royal doggie eyes spotted a strange man with a bag, tip-toeing into the Royal Jewel Room.

That was odd.

ROYAL JEWEL ROOM

ROYAL LOOT

Then, his royal doggie nose sniffed
something absolutely AMAZING:

the **biggest**, smelliest
and most **magnificent** pair of **boots!**

Chips knew he shouldn't,
   but he couldn't help himself.

He just **had** to
have a chew on those
brilliant boots.

But he'd barely started chewing the first boot
when the odd man with a bag tip-toed out of the Royal Jewel Room.

"Oi!" hissed the man.
"Give me back my boot!"

But Chips loved his special boot.
He didn't want to give it back.
Before the man could grab it,
Chips was off in a royal
doggie dash.

The strange man dashed after him. But he hadn't noticed the Royal Chewy Toys that Chips had left in the corridor.

Squeak!

Squonk!

And, **YOW!** **OUCH!** Yikes!

went the man.

*Neeeeeeaay!*

went the toys.

And CRASH! Skitter-scatter! Whoosh!
went the royal jewels, as they spilled
out of the man's bag and tinkled
on to the shiny marble tiles.

All that noise woke the whole palace.
"By Jove!" thundered the Duke.
"He's stealing our jewels.
Officer, seize this scoundrel!"

"And I'd have got away with it, too,"
growled the burglar, "if it wasn't for
that pesky dog chewing my boots!"

"You chewed his boots?"
exclaimed the Duke. "What a clever chap!"

"He chewed his boots!"
cheered everyone. "What a hero!"

"He's simply SPLENDID!" said the Queen. "One shall
arrange a royal parade in Lord Chippington's honour."

It was an excellent parade. But, best of all, the Queen allowed Chips to keep his special boots – and he could chew them whenever he wanted!

For my Marvellous Mum and
for Barney, the best dog, ever!
With love xxx

And a HUGE thank you to the
very wonderful Alison, Zoë,
Pippa and Sophie, for all of
your super creative help
and encouragement.
What a team! x

First published in 2015 by
Alison Green Books
An imprint of Scholastic Children's Books
Euston House, 24 Eversholt Street
London NW1 1DB
A division of Scholastic Ltd
www.scholastic.co.uk
London – New York – Toronto – Sydney
Auckland – Mexico City – New Delhi – Hong Kong

Text & Illustrations copyright © 2015 Kate Leake

HB ISBN: 978-1-407139-34-0
PB ISBN: 978-1-407139-35-7

135798642

Papers used by Scholastic Children's Books are
made from wood grown in sustainable forests.

They were superbly smelly, deliciously disgusting, and, quite simply, jolly well ....

PERFECT.